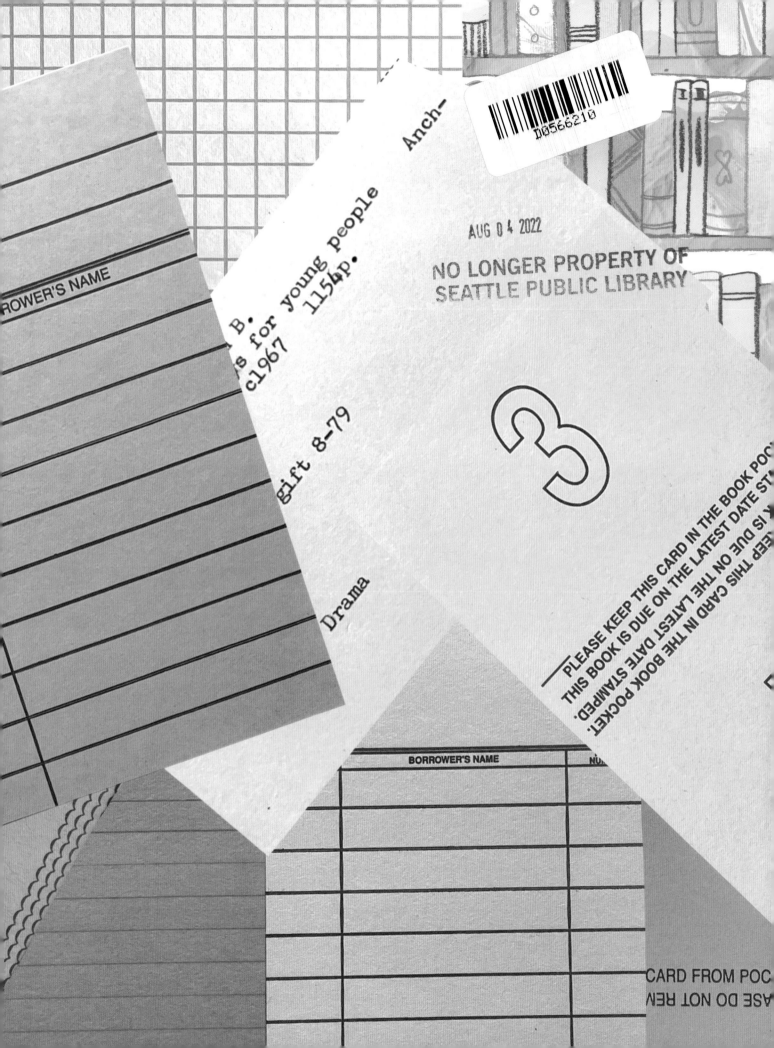

To those who are searching for a place to belong—
and to the members of Sirens NYC who taught me there's a place
for everyone. Heartfelt thanks to Renee Askew, KT Ballantine,
Jen Baquial, Jerry Foster-Julian, Alexandra Hsie, Juanita Kirton,
Alyssa Marko, Annam Hussaini, Andrea Sears, Cheryl Stewart, and—especially—
Kim "Kimasaki" Wetzel (1969–2020). May her memory be a blessing.
—P.D.-S.

To my love and one of my biggest supporters,
Jukabiea K. Barlow
—C.P.B.

Text copyright © 2022 by Pauline David-Sax
Jacket art and interior illustrations copyright © 2022 by Charnelle Pinkney Barlow

All rights reserved. Published in the United States by Doubleday, an imprint of
Random House Children's Books, a division of Penguin Random House LLC, New York.

Doubleday is a registered trademark and the Doubleday colophon is a trademark of Penguin Random House LLC.

Visit us on the Web! rhcbooks.com

Educators and librarians, for a variety of teaching tools, visit us at RHTeachersLibrarians.com

Library of Congress Cataloging-in-Publication Data
Names: David-Sax, Pauline, author. | Pinkney Barlow, Charnelle, illustrator.
Title: Everything in its place : a story of books and belonging / by Pauline David-Sax ; illustrated by Charnelle Pinkney Barlow.
Description: First edition. | New York : Doubleday Books for Young Readers, [2022] | Audience: Ages 5–8.
Summary: "A shy girl who feels most at home in the school library gains the courage to extend herself to others when
she encounters a group of unique, diverse, inspiring women at the diner where her mother works." —Provided by publisher.
Identifiers: LCCN 2021021155 (print) | LCCN 2021021156 (ebook) | ISBN 978-0-593-37882-3 (hardcover) |
ISBN 978-0-593-37883-0 (library binding) | ISBN 978-0-593-37884-7 (ebook)
Subjects: CYAC: Bashfulness—Fiction. | Books and reading—Fiction.
Classification: LCC PZ7.1.D3363 Ev 2022 (print) | LCC PZ7.1.D3363 (ebook) | DDC [E]—dc23

MANUFACTURED IN CHINA
10 9 8 7 6 5 4 3 2 1
First Edition

Everything
in Its
Place

A Story of Books and Belonging

by Pauline David-Sax

illustrated by Charnelle Pinkney Barlow

Doubleday Books for Young Readers

"Listen to the trees talking in their sleep," she whispered,

"What nice dreams they must have!"

The bell rings and I push open the library door.

The book-return bin is full.

Got your work cut out for you, Nicky, Ms. Gillam says.

I gather the books in my arms

and give them a hug.

Welcome home, I whisper.

I head down the rows of numbered shelves

to put them back where they belong.

The sounds of recess waft through the open window.

Everyone's found their group:

the soccer players,

the jump-ropers,

the kids who love hopscotch.

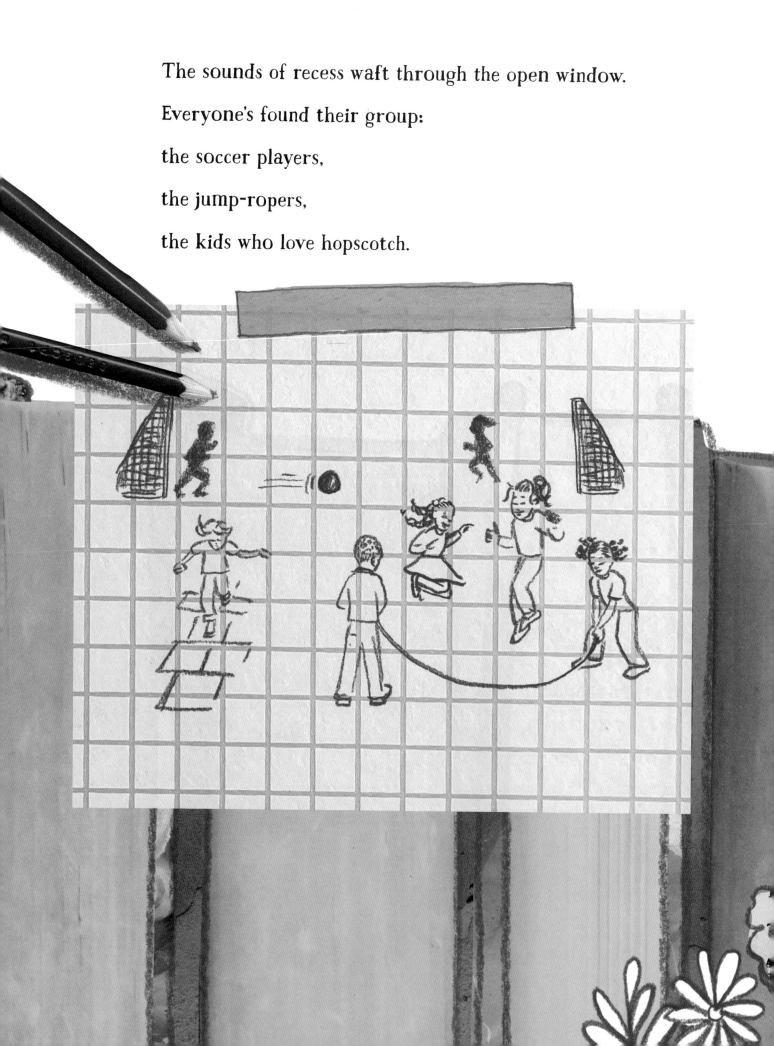

You want to go outside to play?

Ms. Gillam asks

like she always does

when she sees me watching

and I shake my head

like I always do

and get back to the books.

Who needs recess

when you can reshelve books?

I walk up and down the aisles,

each book's special number telling me where to go.

Astronomy—520s.

The Ancient World—930s.

Everything has its place in the library.

The books. Ms. Gillam. Me.

flower arrangements

exhibiting flower

.Y. Crowell [1968]

.)

nows I.Title
ats

45.92

History

745.54
K

938

MATHEM

10.03
NI

The Uni PB

MISSISSIPPI-FICT

540.

Taylor, M

I'm almost done when Ms. Gillam tells me her news.

A conference for librarians! she exclaims. *A whole week!*

I try to smile but all I can think is

A whole week of recess

and my stomach starts to hurt.

It's still hurting after school when I get to Cathy's Café.

Cathy is Mama and Thursday is pecan pie

but today I'm not hungry at all.

At least here it's all right to be alone.

Like Mr. Williams,

who orders his chicken soup extra hot

so he can close his eyes

and breathe in the steam.

And Mrs. D,

who tucks her paper napkin

carefully into her blouse

before she eats her tuna on rye.

Pecan Pie 3.99

Apple Pie 4.99

My favorite is Maggie:

short hair,

scruffy clothes

(just like me),

fork in one hand,

book in the other,

as she eats Mama's pie.

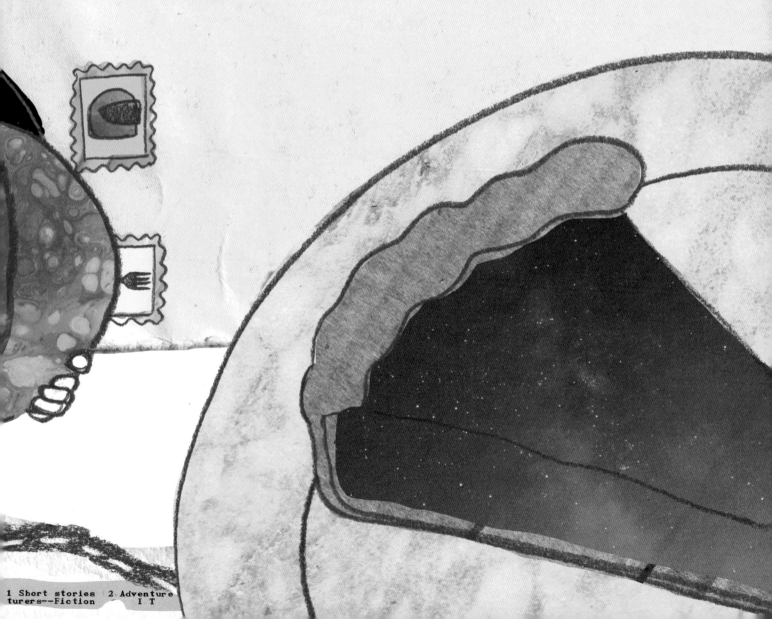

When Maggie finishes reading something good,

she lends it to me.

Today it's a book of poetry (800s).

Thanks, I say. I tuck it in my bag.

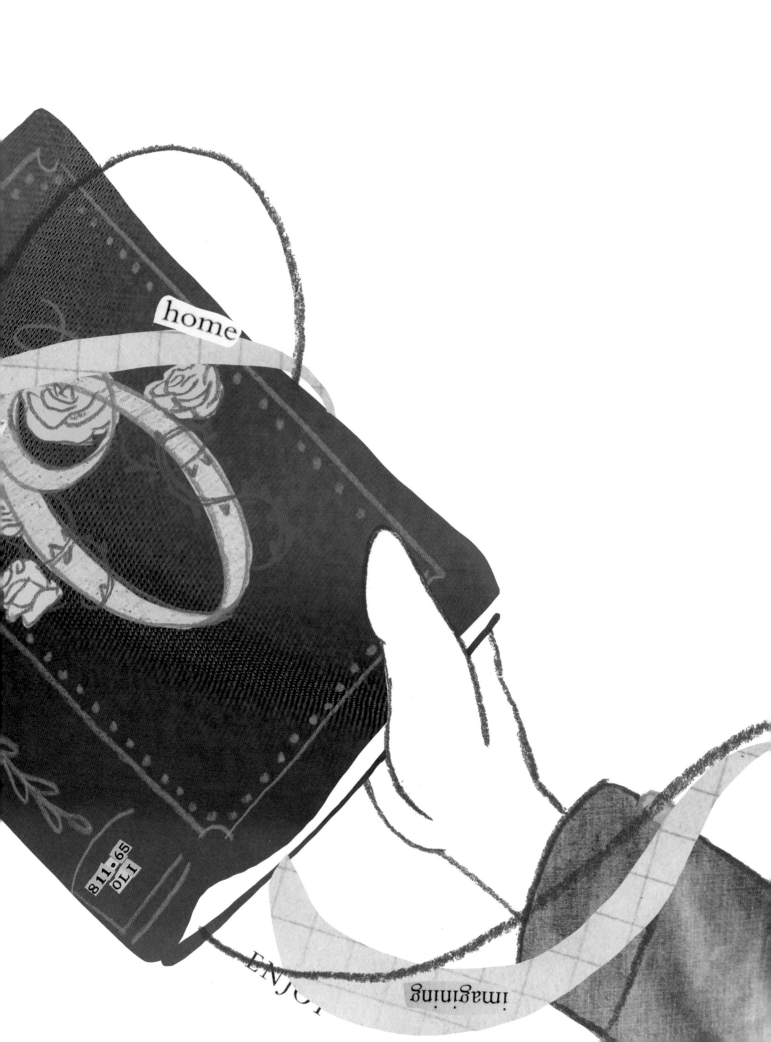

home

ENJOY

imagining

811.65
OLI

I watch Maggie head outside

and start up her motorcycle.

I asked her once,

Isn't it scary?

But she said,

Everything in life is a risk,

and whenever I see her on her bike

she looks so happy,

so alive,

so free.

Next day's Friday.

Maybe it'll be good for you, Ms. Gillam says.

Hang out with kids your own age.

I pretend to be really interested in fossils (560s)

so she won't see my eyes fill with tears.

On Saturday I'm back at the café

helping Mama

when I hear a noise outside.

Like Maggie's bike, only louder.

I take a look and see

a fleet of motorcycles

rumbling into the parking lot.

A dozen at least,

all different colors,

shapes,

sizes.

butter

sugar

cup flour

And when Maggie walks in,
she's not alone,
but followed by
a group of women,
helmets in hands.

Cathy, Maggie says.

Told my sisters so much about your pie
they just had to try it for themselves.

I'm confused. *Sisters?*

Like the bikes,

they are all different colors,

shapes,

sizes.

Maggie laughs at my puzzled look.

Motorcycle sisters, she says.

And I see each jacket

has the same patch,

each face

the same smile.

I watch them

in wonder:

all so different,

but together, too.

Trading laughs

and bites of pie,

looking so happy,

so alive,

so free.

When the recess bell rings on Monday,

I follow the other kids outside

on heavy feet,

watching as they divide

into their noisy groups.

I stand against a wall
and dig into my bag
for something to read.
I find Maggie's book.
Poems by Mary Oliver.

There's one called "Wild Geese"

about feeling lost

and I read it again and again,

wondering what it means.

I wish Maggie were here

or Ms. Gillam

but they're not.

A shadow crosses the page

and I look up.

It's a girl,

one of the hopscotchers

or jump-ropers,

only she's not hopping or jumping,

she's standing next to me.

I love poetry, she says,

pointing to my book,

and although I don't know her,

I remember Maggie's sisters

and that *everything in life is a risk*

and I say,

Me too.

And we lean against the wall together
and read.

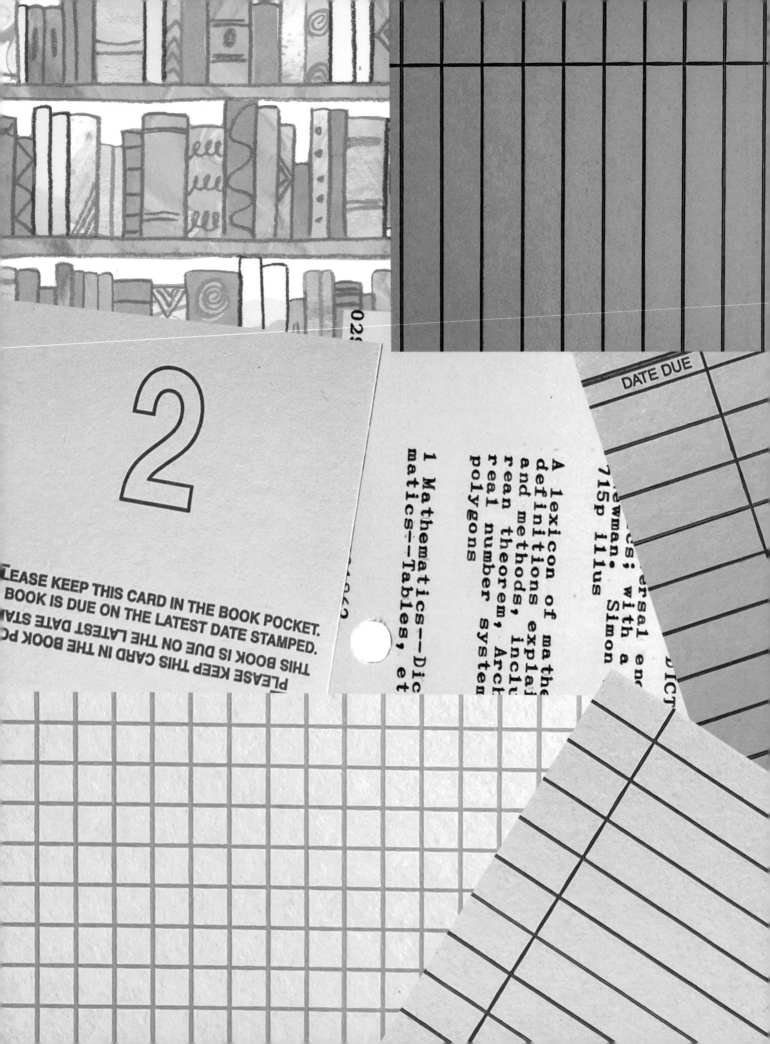